My Sister is a Witch!

First published in 2006 by
Franklin Watts
338 Euston Road
London
NW1 3BH

Franklin Watts Australia
Level 17/207 Kent Street
Sydney
NSW 2000

A CIP catalogue record for this book is available
from the British Library.

ISBN: 978 0 7496 6898 3

Series Editor: Jackie Hamley
Series Advisor: Dr Hilary Minns
Series Designer: Peter Scoulding

Printed in China

Franklin Watts is a division of
Hachette Children's Books,
an Hachette UK company.
www.hachette.co.uk

My Sister
is a Witch!

by Joan Stimson

Illustrated by Jan Lewis

FRANKLIN WATTS
LONDON•SYDNEY

Joan Stimson

"I think the best thing about being a witch would be riding a broomstick – VROOM! VROOM!"

Jan Lewis

"It's magic to draw and I'd like to draw more. I'd love to make spells but perhaps not the smells!"

My sister is a witch.

5

You can tell by her hat.

You can tell by her cat.

My sister is a witch.

You can tell
by the smell
when she's
making a spell.

11

My sister is a witch.

13

You can tell
by the VROOM

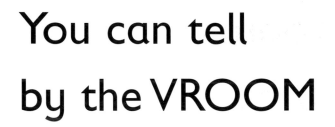

as she zooms
on her broom.

My sister is a witch.

She's hairy and scary.

19

But just for today,
my sister is a witch ...

... and we're going to play!

Notes for adults

TADPOLES is structured to provide support for newly independent readers. The stories may also be used by adults for sharing with young children.

Starting to read alone can be daunting. **TADPOLES** helps by providing visual support and repeating words and phrases. These books will both develop confidence and encourage reading and rereading for pleasure.

If you are reading this book with a child, here are a few suggestions:

1. Make reading fun! Choose a time to read when you and the child are relaxed and have time to share the story.

2. Talk about the story before you start reading. Look at the cover and the blurb. What might the story be about? Why might the child like it?

3. Encourage the child to reread the story, and to retell the story in their own words, using the illustrations to remind them what has happened.

4. Discuss the story and see if the child can relate it to their own experience, or perhaps compare it to another story they know.

5. Give praise! Remember that small mistakes need not always be corrected.

If you enjoyed this book, why not try another **TADPOLES** story?